3

The Tricks of Master Dabble

To Kaethe,
Heidi,
Rachel

The Tricks of Master Dabble

by Harve Zemach

Illustrated by Margot Zemach

Holt, Rinehart and Winston

New York · Chicago · San Francisco

Once upon a time, in a faraway country, a king and a queen lived in a castle, and they had a hundred servants. There were servants abovestairs, and servants belowstairs, and there were servants backstairs, too. And one was a boy called Andrew, whose job was: to look after the queen's canaries in the morning, and to fetch things and fix things all afternoon for the lords and ladies of the court, and at night to peel onions for the king's soup. Andrew enjoyed his morning work, and he didn't mind the afternoons, but he hated peeling onions. It always made him weep, and he longed to be given something different to do. He didn't know what, but something different anyway.

There came a day when he got his wish. A stranger arrived at the castle, a stranger with a ragged cloak hanging from his bony shoulders. He said his name was Dabble—Master Dabble—and that he possessed a rare skill. He could paint pictures, he said, so lifelike and true that nobody could tell the difference between them and the real things.

He was brought before the king, and the king said, "Master Dabble, the Queen and I are very fond of birds. If you paint us a picture of birds that look real enough to fly, we shall give you a sack of gold."

"Very well, Your Majesty," replied Master Dabble, "but it will take time and care. The last time I painted a picture of birds, they looked real enough to peck, but not quite real enough to fly. But that was many years ago and I have since improved. I only ask that I be allowed to work without interruption until the painting is done, and that you give me an assistant to see that I have whatever I need."

"Certainly," said the king. He looked about and saw Andrew. "Andrew, take Master Dabble to the East Hall, upon whose wall he shall paint a picture of birds, and see to it that he has everything he needs."

So Andrew showed Master Dabble to the East Hall and asked him what he would need.

The artist looked around the Hall, and he pushed open a window to let in fresh air. Then he peeked out into the corridor, to the right and to the left, and when he saw that they were alone, he grasped Andrew by both hands and said, "Need? My boy, I need food! And drink! Drink is what I need! I need the best food and drink you can find! So off you go to the kitchen, and don't forget to take some for yourself!"

Andrew went to the kitchen and got the best food and drink he could find, and took some for himself.

Master Dabble ate as if he had not tasted food for a year. He ate his fill and he drank his fill, and then he fell asleep.

The next morning the artist called for a big break-
fast, after which he went for a stroll in the garden. He
returned carrying a peacock feather which he had found
entangled in a bush. Then he drank quite a lot of wine
with his lunch and sang songs afterward, while strum-
ming on a battered lute. And he spent all evening telling
Andrew stories of his travels and adventures.

Not a spot of paint did he mix; never a brush did he
lift; not a line did he draw.

Soon Andrew could see that the wall of the East
Hall was not getting painted. When the next day passed

the same way, and the next, and the next, and Master Dabble still had not begun his work, Andrew grew worried. He wondered what would happen when the time came to show the king his picture.

At last he could not resist asking Master Dabble about it. "Sir," he said, "when are you going to paint the picture of birds? And can I help? If you mixed some blue paint, do you think I could make some sky for a background?"

Master Dabble frowned. "Interested in painting, are you?" he asked.

Andrew said he was, although he had never done it before. He certainly itched to try.

"Forget it!" said Master Dabble. "It's a hard life, being a painter of pictures, very hard. All those colors and shapes; much too confusing for a boy like you. Just talking about it has made me tired and I shall have to take a nap."

Pretty soon a messenger came with a message from the queen, saying that she was eager to see the painting of birds, and when would it be done?

The artist replied that it was too soon, that the birds were not yet perfect to the tip of the last feather, that they looked real enough to peck and real enough to sing and real enough to flutter their wings, but not yet real enough to fly.

And so some more time passed, and still Master Dabble just ate and drank and strolled in the garden and sang songs and snored. But then the king wouldn't wait any longer. Attended by the lords and ladies of the court, and with the queen carrying her silver cage of canaries, the royal party arrived at the East Hall.

Andrew flung open the door. Everyone could see the wall, as unpainted as ever before. And there was Master Dabble, leaning out the window and waving his arms.

"Too late, too late!" he cried, coming away from the window and stamping his foot. "All my work has gone to waste!"

The king was astonished. "Where are the birds, Master Dabble?" he asked.

"Ah, the birds!" Master Dabble sighed. "They were so beautiful, absolutely perfect, real as life to the tip of the last feather."

"But where . . . ?" asked the king.

Suddenly Master Dabble thrust out his arm and pointed a trembling finger at Andrew. "There!" he cried. "There's the one who did it. This worthless boy *knew* that the birds were real enough to fly, but he went right ahead and opened that window; and so, of course,

they all flew out, one after another, flapping like mad!"

Andrew was thunderstruck. "I tried my best," he heard Master Dabble say. "I tried to stop them, but it was too late. There is nothing left but this."

He held up a feather, one brightly colored feather.

Well, Andrew tried to say it wasn't true, but everyone could see that the feather was real, and so they believed Master Dabble. The king gave Andrew a good scolding and sent him down to the kitchen to peel onions all day long—morning, afternoon, and night. And oh! How it made him weep!

Master Dabble in the meantime scowled and pounded his fist and demanded his sack of gold, because it wasn't his fault that the picture had flown away. The king did not know what to do, but the queen had an idea.

"Master Dabble," she said, "perhaps you will stay a while longer and paint another picture for us."

Master Dabble's scowl changed instantly to a smile. "Since you request it, dear lady," he said, "I cannot refuse. What shall it be this time? A battle scene so lifelike and true that one can hear the shouts and clash of swords?"

"Oh, no!" cried the queen, "that would be too fearsome!"

"Then how about a picture of a garden looking so real that the whole castle will be filled with the smell of flowers?"

"No, no," declared the king. "Flowers make me sneeze."

"Or . . . ," said Master Dabble, "or shall it be a grand portrait of the courtiers, showing each noble lord and lady just exactly as he or she really is? Ah, *that* would be a picture!"

The queen was delighted, and the king was pleased, and the courtiers felt very proud that they were going to

have their pictures painted. Even the canaries twittered loudly. And so cunning Master Dabble locked himself up again in the East Hall, coming out only for long strolls in the garden and to take his meals at the king's own table. He told everyone about the grand portrait he was painting—how large and lifesize it was, and how difficult was the work.

Each evening at dinner he would explain what he had been doing that day, saying things like: "Today I began on the figure of the Duke of Dimlit, and completed painting the top of his head." (Whereupon the Duke of Dimlit, who was bald, nervously dabbed at the top of his head with his napkin.)

Another evening Master Dabble announced: "Today I have painted one-half of Countess Thelma of Thump, and it used up so much of my paint that I shall have to mix more tomorrow." (Everyone around the table laughed, except Countess Thelma of Thump, who was extremely fat.)

Very soon the courtiers began to visit Master Dabble in secret, one by one, late at night, standing outside the East Hall and whispering through the door.

The Duke of Dimlit was the first. "Master Dabble!" he whispered, "paint my likeness, if you wish, but I must ask you to add some hair to my head. It is not fitting for a Duke to be seen all bald in a picture!"

"Oh, what a shameful request!" exclaimed the artist. "I promised the King and Queen to paint everyone as he really looks. And you, sir, look entirely bald."

But then Master Dabble added, lowering his voice, "If you leave me your purse, and say not a word to anyone, I promise to make you look fine and handsome, even though bald."

The Duke of Dimlit unfastened his purse, heavy with coins, left it before the door, and returned to his chambers.

Next came Countess Thelma of Thump. "Master Dabble!" she whispered, "paint my likeness, if you must, but a little less large than lifesize, or I shall refuse to look at your picture!"

"Too bad. I should like you to see my picture," replied Master Dabble, "but I cannot do otherwise than what I have promised the King and Queen, which is to paint you as you really are, and you really are extremely large. However, if you leave me your jewels, and say not a word to anyone, I promise to make you look charming and beautiful, even though very large."

Countess Thelma of Thump slipped off her jeweled necklace and twisted the rings from her fingers, leaving them in a heap at Master Dabble's door.

Some time later Baron Bull the Bold appeared, standing on tiptoe to reach the keyhole and whispering fiercely, "Dabble! Don't you dare paint me shorter than befits a soldier and a gentleman!"

"I am to paint you as you are, sir," replied Master Dabble. "And you are ridiculously short, sir! But do not despair. If you leave me your sword, and say not a word to anyone, I promise to make you look proud and ferocious, even though short."

"Not my sword, Dabble! My coat, my boots, anything, but not my sword!"

"Your sword!" said Master Dabble.

So Baron Bull the Bold gave up his sword and slunk away.

It wasn't long before the abovestairs servants discovered all these nightly comings and goings. And they told the backstairs servants, who in turn told the servants belowstairs. And one day the saddest boy in the kitchen, Andrew the onion-peeler, heard the whole story from a scullery maid.

"Are you sure," asked Andrew, blowing his nose and squinting through red-rimmed eyes, "that Master Dabble says he is painting them lifesize and exactly the way they really look?"

"That's what they say," replied the scullery maid.

"And has anyone seen the picture?"

"Not yet," said she, "because it is covered by a

cloth. But now Master Dabble says it is finished, and this afternoon it will be shown."

"This afternoon!" Andrew jumped up, threw away a half-peeled onion, tore off his apron, and rushed out of the kitchen.

The scullery maid had not been mistaken. That very afternoon the king and queen and the duke and the countess and the baron marched to the East Hall to be shown the grand portrait. Master Dabble met them at the door.

At his request everyone entered and took up positions in proper order and rank in front of the west wall, which was covered by a curtain of heavy cloth. With a flourish Master Dabble swept the curtain open and quickly stepped aside.

Lo! there were all the lords and ladies, posed in proper order and rank, looking exactly lifelike and real, just like mirror images of themselves.

"Truly a remarkable likeness!" exclaimed the queen. "The figures seem almost alive! Why, if I can believe my eyes, the figure of the Duke of Dimlit just now wagged its bald head!"

"Bald I may be," muttered the Duke of Dimlit, "but it is true that the fellow has made me look very fine and handsome. There I stand, looking fine and handsome indeed, alongside the large Countess Thelma of Thump."

"Well!" gasped Countess Thelma, "Master Dabble has not made me any smaller, but he has certainly made me look more charming and beautiful than ever, as he promised he would. And speaking of small, just look at Baron Bull the Bold!"

"I'll admit there are some in that picture taller than myself," the Baron remarked, "but none so wondrously proud and ferocious!"

Then Master Dabble began to pull the curtain closed again, saying there were one or two spots of paint

not quite dry and he wouldn't want anyone to lean against it and soil his clothes. But suddenly there was a commotion in the rear of the Hall.

"My canaries!" cried the queen. "My canaries have gotten loose! Catch them, someone!"

The queen's nine canaries flew wildly around the room. It was Andrew, of course, who had brought the cage to the Hall and let them loose. Now he came charging down the Hall waving a long pole with a net at the end. One canary flew straight toward the picture, and Andrew went after it, giving a mighty swing with the pole.

The queen shrieked.

CRACK! CRASH! There was glass all over the floor. And the painting was gone.

(In fact, it had not been a painting at all, but a large mirror that Master Dabble had fixed upon the wall.)

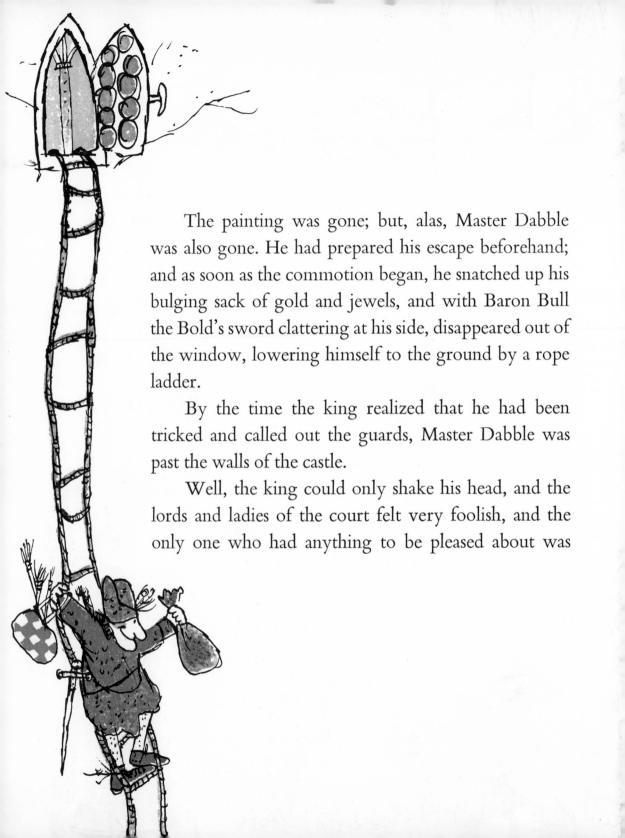

The painting was gone; but, alas, Master Dabble was also gone. He had prepared his escape beforehand; and as soon as the commotion began, he snatched up his bulging sack of gold and jewels, and with Baron Bull the Bold's sword clattering at his side, disappeared out of the window, lowering himself to the ground by a rope ladder.

By the time the king realized that he had been tricked and called out the guards, Master Dabble was past the walls of the castle.

Well, the king could only shake his head, and the lords and ladies of the court felt very foolish, and the only one who had anything to be pleased about was

Andrew. So when all the broken glass was finally swept away and when the queen's canaries were safely back in their cage, the king called Andrew to him. He said he was sorry for not believing him the first time and asked the boy what he would like for a reward.

"Your Majesty," said Andrew, who had his answer all ready, "I would like to have my old job of looking after the canaries in the morning. And I would like not to have to peel onions anymore—not even at night. And by your leave, I would like to learn to paint pictures in the afternoon—real ones, full of colors and shapes and blue skies and birds and people."

"Very well," said the king. "You shall become Master Andrew, the painter. But I command you, Master Andrew, never to paint pictures like those of Master Dabble, pictures so lifelike and true that nobody can tell the difference between them and the real things."

And Andrew—Master Andrew—promised that he would not.